A CONTRARY LITTLE QUAIL

JANE THAYER

illustrated by
Meg Wohlberg

William Morrow and Company New York

First there was an egg,
a cold cold, wet wet egg,
alone in a nest.
"A quail's egg," somebody said.
"Let's take it home," somebody else said.
They put the egg under a lamp
on the kitchen shelf.

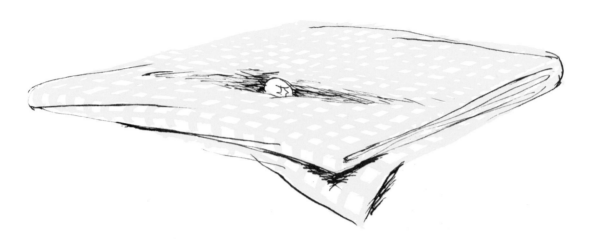

"It certainly won't hatch," they said.
But something was certainly pecking away,
peck, peck, peck.
"It can't come out that end of the egg.
That's the wrong end," they said.
But out the wrong end
stepped a tiny quail, wobbly and wet.
"Hello, Annabel!" they said.
Annabel saw Mr. and Mrs. Lee,
and naturally she thought
they were her parents.
Mr. and Mrs. Lee put down
some chick seed and water,
and left her alone to dry out.

Annabel plopped down to the floor,
picked herself up,
and set off on her wobbly, wet legs.
"Here she comes to find us!"
Mrs. Lee exclaimed.
"I found you!" said Annabel
with a happy chirp.
"She looks like a bumblebee on stilts,"
said Mr. Lee.

Annabel held tight to Mr. Lee's finger
while he smoothed her tiny feathers.
"We'll have to let her go
as soon as she can fly," said Mrs. Lee.
"Of course," said Mr. Lee.
In came the white cat Colfax.
"Don't be afraid of Colfax,"
Mrs. Lee said.
Annabel wasn't.
"This is Annabel, Colfax.
Mind your manners," Mr. Lee told him.
Colfax said OK, if he had to.

Annabel, as big as a bumblebee,
followed her parents about.
When dinner time came
she said she would like to sit
at the table.
Mrs. Lee brought a high chair.
"Will you have some chick seed?"
Mrs. Lee said.
Annabel wouldn't.
She was a contrary little quail.

"I prefer sauerkraut," she said,
"or spiders, or whatever you're having."
She had four helpings of sauerkraut
and fell asleep at the table.
She didn't wake up
when they put her to bed
on a warm wool scarf.
Mr. and Mrs. Lee looked down
at Annabel, sleeping.
"It will be quite a while
before we can let her go," said Mr. Lee.
"Quite a while," said his wife.
They tiptoed out.

Next morning Annabel chirped with joy
when she woke up and saw them.
"Chick seed?" said Mrs. Lee.
"Orange juice," said Annabel.
She had orange juice.
"We won't put her in a cage,"
Mrs. Lee said.
"Oh no, she's a wild quail.
She must be free," said her husband.
People looked at Annabel
and solemnly said, "She may not live."
But she did.

She looked more like a quail now.
As Annabel grew up
she helped with the work,
gobbling up spiders and dust.
She was loving and sweet
and excellent company.
She played double solitaire with Mr. Lee.
She watched TV.
She helped Mrs. Lee with her sewing.
She cuddled up to the white cat Colfax,
who purred.
She was gracious to all.

When company came she rushed to the door,
saying, "How *do* you do?"
and asked Mrs. Lee
please to bring tea and cake.
Wild quail sometimes waddled
through the garden,
whole families of them,
and called to her to come out:
Bob white! Bob white!
Annabel shivered and stayed indoors
with people and hot-water heat.

When she was almost grown
Mrs. Lee said one day,
"We love you, Annabel.
We'd like you to stay.
But you are a little wild quail.
Come out in the garden.
You may fly away if you want to."
"Why?" said Annabel contrarily.

She took a bath in the dirt,
wallowing and shaking her feathers,
while Mrs. Lee stood guard.
She hurried back to the house
and the hot-water heat.

One day when Annabel was taking
a bath in the dirt,
with Mrs. Lee on guard,
she heard outside the fence,
Chatter, chatter.
Mrs. Lee went to look
and brought back a baby squirrel.
"Poor little thing," she said.
"He fell out of the nest."

They went into the house,
and Mrs. Lee held the squirrel on her lap.
Annabel flew up too.
Mr. Lee took the little squirrel.
Annabel lighted on his shoulder
and ruffled her feathers rudely.
"You're not jealous of Colfax,
so why are you jealous
of a little squirrel?" Mr. Lee said.
But Annabel, being contrary, was.
She flip-flopped and scolded.

Mr. and Mrs. Lee
fed the little squirrel warm milk.
They made a bed in a box.
They didn't forget Annabel,
but they were busy.
Annabel stamped her foot.
"Annabel dear, you're upset,"
said Mrs. Lee.
"Come have a lovely dirt bath
to make you feel better."
Annabel was wallowing,
to calm her hurt feelings,
with Mrs. Lee on guard,
when she heard *Chatter, chatter.*
"There's the mother squirrel,"
said Mrs. Lee.
She put the little squirrel in the woods
where his mother came and got him.

Annabel gave a joyful squawk
when that squirrel was gone.
She flew up on Mrs. Lee's shoulder
and cuddled close.
"You want all the attention, you wretch,"
said Mrs. Lee lovingly.
Annabel smiled.
Next, the Lees' grandson, Sammy, came.
The Lees played games with him
and held him on their laps.
"Don't you like little boys?"
Mrs. Lee asked Annabel.
Annabel went under the bed.

Finally Sammy went home.
Annabel came out, squawking with joy,
and flew up on Mr. Lee's head.

"You're a contrary little quail,"
said Mr. Lee.
She smiled.
Then the Lees' son, Luther,
came home from college.
This was worse than having
a squirrel or a Sammy around
because the Lees seemed so delighted.
Luther played double solitaire
with his father.
Annabel walked around,
muddling up cards.

He watched TV with his mother.

Annabel flapped.

He held Colfax on his lap,

and Colfax purred.

Annabel was hopping mad.

Luther tried to be friendly.

He said "Hi."

She turned her back.

She waited and waited for him to go away,

but he didn't go.

And one day,
when she was being ignored,
Annabel stamped her foot
in the roast-beef gravy.
"Why, Annabel *Lee!*" cried Mrs. Lee.
"Luther is going to live here too.
You be good!" Mr. Lee said.
Never had anyone said
a cross word to Annabel before.
She flew into a corner,
hunched up her feathers,
and thought dark thoughts.
She thought, They don't like me.
They like that Luther.

I'll fly far, far away and live with birds!
She went to the door.
"It's cold and it's going to rain,"
said Mrs. Lee.
"You don't want a bath."
"Yes, I do," said Annabel.
She wallowed in the dirt.
Suddenly she flip-flopped over the fence.
"Don't go too far away," Mrs. Lee called.
So Annabel flew farther away,
smiling with satisfaction.

"Now I'm far, far away,
and I'm going to live with birds
and never go home," she said.
When she saw
a flock of wild quail feeding,
she flew down
and said she was going to live with them.
The wild quail
weren't keen about taking in
a quail they didn't know.
They talked it over with some excitement,
and word got around
that a stranger was in the woods.
Suddenly the trees were full of birds,
screaming at this stranger.
They flew overhead.
Caw! Caw! Yaw! Yaw! Whoo!
Bob white! Bob white!

Annabel was scared to death
and scurried under a tree.
The wind rose and ruffled her feathers.
Then she saw a friend,
stepping along and peering at her.
How glad she was to see a cat.
Over she ran.
But this was a strange cat, not Colfax.
When she joyfully looked him in the eye
she didn't like what she saw.
Annabel flip-flopped in alarm
and just in time flew out of reach
of the cat's sharp claws.

She clung to a tree,
her heart pounding.
Soon she felt drops of rain.
The rain became icy streams
that poured down
Annabel's feathers.
She shut her eyes and clung.
Night came.

Annabel clung to the tree all night,
surrounded by enemies and unfriendly eyes.
She was cold, wet,
and too frightened to move.
She thought daylight would never come,
but finally it did.
The other birds had kept warm and dry,
but Annabel, used to hot-water heat,
felt nearly frozen.
She had one thought now—to get home.
But which way was it?
Annabel flew down to the ground
on her cold, stiff wings
and scurried this way and that.
Then, faint and far away,
she heard, "Annabel!"

She flew toward the sound of her name
and landed in the garden
where Mr. and Mrs. Lee, Luther,
and the white cat Colfax
were anxiously looking and looking.
"We thought you had gone
to live with birds!" Mrs. Lee cried.
"Oh, no!" said Annabel.
She cuddled up to Mrs. Lee,
then Mr. Lee, then Colfax, who purred.

She looked up at Luther
and ruffled her feathers.
"Mind your manners, Annabel.
He's here to stay," Colfax advised.
Annabel flew into a corner,
hunched up her feathers,
and thought very deep thoughts.
"She's going to be difficult again,"
said Mr. Lee.
"Come in and get warm, Annabel."
Annabel was hunched up, thinking.
"What are we going to do?"
said Mrs. Lee in dismay.
"Please come in the house, Annabel."
Annabel kept on thinking.
Suddenly, up she flew
and landed on Luther's head.